Wallace & Gromit ™

AND THE LOST SLIPPER

Text by **Tristan Davies**

Drawings by **Nick Newman**

Hodder & Stoughton

Copyright © 1997 Wallace and Gromit Ltd and Nick Newman and Tristan Davies
based on original characters created by Nick Park Character © and registered trademark
Wallace and Gromit Ltd and Aardman Animations Ltd

Lettering by Gary Gilbert

First published in Great Britain in 1997
by Hodder & Stoughton
A division of Hodder Headline PLC

A CIP catalogue record for this title is available from the British Library.

ISBN 0 340 69655 9
Printed in Belgium by Proost International Book Production

Hodder and Stoughton
A division of Hodder Headline PLC
338 Euston Road
London NW1 3BH

As the stars of any animated film would tell you if they could, being an animated character can be very frustrating. You spend long periods of time moving very, very slowly, millimetre by millimetre, for the cameras. And then in between films you spend long periods of time not moving at all while resting on the shelf in your creator's studio.

Wallace and Gromit, with their huge appetite for life and high-protein dairy products, refused to take all this lying down lying down. They cried out, albeit completely silently, to be let loose in exciting new cheesy adventures. And because both characters have legs, as they say – four in Gromit's case, even though he often only walks on two of them – I was delighted to allow the pair to stretch them across the printed page.

I do hope you enjoy *The Lost Slipper* and *The Curse of the Ramsbottoms*, the first two stories in a series of new comic strip adventures for Wallace and Gromit, as much as they enjoyed not having to gather dust resting up on that shelf in the Aardman studio.

Nick Park

Aardman Animations Ltd Directors: Peter Lord, David Sproxton and Nick Park
Gas Ferry Road Bristol BS1 6UN England
Tel: 0117 984 8485 Fax: 0117 984 8486 http://www.aardman.com
Registered Office Address as above Registered in England and Wales Registration number: 2050843
VAT Registration number: GB 609 3011 72

DRAMATIS PERSONAE
(Which according to Gromit's written translation,
is Latin for 'whom you are about to receive')

WALLACE
Inventor, handyman, cheese-fancier – and for the purposes of this story, a man who has lost his slipper but not his marbles.

GROMIT
Constant companion, housekeeper and dog – Gromit does all the doggy things you'd expect: he sits, he stays, he does algebra in his head while speed-knitting.

WILLIAM THE CONQUEROR
A conqueror from Normandy, called William, whose subjugation of the Anglo-Saxon people is a piece of cake compared to all the dreadful meals he is forced to eat in England.

BARON WALLAIS DE WALLAIS
Inventor, handyman and convicted coiffeur, this Norman ancestor was years ahead of his time when he tunnelled out of a French prison cell and under the Channel to England. Sadly, history only remembers him for his use of small furry animals with sharp teeth while trying to perfect a do-it-yourself medieval pudding basin haircutting system. It did not catch on.

UG-WALLACE
Inventor, handyman and non-shaver, this even more distant forebear held the world land speed rollerblading record (uncontested) in One Millicn Years B.C. A celebrated wit and conversationalist – if your idea of a good conversation involves going 'Ug-ug-ug' a lot.

WALLACE'S GREAT-GREAT-GREAT NEPHEW
Inventor, handyman and hopping mad eco-warrior, Great-Great-Great Uncle Wallace's future relative has a bee in his baseball cap about families who drive more than one pair of clogs.

THE PHARAOHS
Ancient Egyptians, sandal-wearers and confirmed cat-lovers, there's not much to say about Queen Neferti-tea-for-two-tu-tankha-etc. – except that it's much simpler just to call them Mr and Mrs Pharaoh.

CRIKEY, PREPARE TO REPEL BURROWERS, GROMIT.

CRUMBLING COURGETTES!

BONJOUR TOUT LE MONDE! FREEDOM AT LAST FROM MY FRENCH PRISON CELL! OÙ AM I EXACTLY?

IN AN *ENGLISH* PRISON CELL, CHUCK.

UNDERGROUND MAP
YE NORMAN LINE

SACRÉ-DRAT! IT SEEMS I'VE INVENTED SOME KIND OF FIXED LINK SHUTTLE FROM MAINLAND EUROPE WITH SERVICES ON THE MILLENNIUM. NOBODY'S EVER GOING TO WANT THAT.

PERMIT-NOUS TO INTRODUCE OURSELVES. BARON WALLAIS DE WALLAIS, INVENTOR EXTRAORDINAIRE, AND MY TRUSTY HOUND, GROMIT-LE-CHIEN.

BY 'ECK YOU LOOK FAMILIAR...

I KNOW! YOU'RE ONE THERMAL CHAIN-MAIL SOCK SHORT OF A MATCHING PAIR! QUEL COINCIDENCE!

WE'RE ON THE TRAIL OF AN EVIL MEDIEVAL TIME-TRAVELLING FOOTWEAR THIEF AND NO MISTAKE!

LATER THAT DAY...

...AND I WAS JAILED FOR MY MOST INFLUENTIAL INVENTION YET...

...THE MEDIEVAL PUDDING BASIN HAIRCUTTER WITH SELF-TRIMMING STOAT-OF-THE-ART FRINGE SYSTEM.

THE CHOICE OF STYLES WAS SO POPULAR THEY PUT ME IN PRISON FOR MY OWN SAFETY.

THAT'S ALL VERY WELL, BUT WITH FOUR TO A CELL WE'LL HAVE TO START STRETCHING OUR RATIONS.

OH YES. I'VE GOT HIM WELL TRAINED.

S·T·R·E·T·C·H

VERY INTERESTING -- BUT WE FRENCH WILL NEVER SWALLOW IT. I, HOWEVER, KNOW JUST WHAT TO DO WITH YOUR SO-CALLED *ENGLISH* 'FRENCH STICK'.........

GULP!

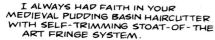

FINDING MY SLIPPER NOW IS GOING TO BE A MAMMOTH, ER, TUSK. WE'D BETTER SET UP OUR BASE CAMP.

MAKE YOURSELF USEFUL WHILE I ERECT THE DORMOVANCAMPMOBILETENTETTE WITH ENSUITE FACILITIES.

ER-LAP!

THIS IS NO TIME TO BURY BONES, LAD.

MIND YOU HE IS ONLY A DOG, I SUPPOSE.

WELL DONE, GROMIT. VERY 'BONES & GARDENS'. WE'LL HAVE A CAMP-WARMING WITH THE LAST OF OUR CHEDDAR.

MEN   DOGS

BEWARE OF THE MAN

HUNGRY HUMANOIDS! THE AROMA OF MELTING CHEESE HAS ATTRACTED COMPANY. D'YOU THINK HE'S HAD HIS TEA?

UG!

UG UG UG. UG UG UG. OG!

HE'S AFTER OUR TUCK. HE'S PROBABLY NEVER SEEN A FLAME-GRILLED CHEESE TOASTIE BEFORE.

UG UG UG. UG UG UG. OG!

NOW DON'T TRY ANY MONKEY BUSINESS WITH ME, MATE, OR YOU'LL BE HEARING FROM MY D-OG.

YOU'D BETTER LOOK OUT OR YOU'LL BURN YOUR FINGERS IN THE--

?

O-O-O-O-O-O-O

...A-A-A-A-A-G-H-H!!

THAT'S THE TROUBLE WITH BONE AGE MAN; TOTALLY BONE-HEADED ABOUT NEW TECHNOLOGY.

D-OG. D-OG. D-OG.

GROMIT'S A D-OG ALL RIGHT. AND NOW IF YOU'RE FEELING BETTER YOU CAN HELP HIM FIND MY SLIPPER.

READING HIS BODY LANGUAGE, I'LL TAKE THAT AS AN 'UG'.

WEEKS OF RECUPERATION LATER...

THESE EARLY ROLLERBLADES ARE LETHAL. I MUST INVENT A MEANS OF SLOWING THEM DOWN.

A NAVIGATIONAL, GRAVITATIONAL, OVERSHOOT PARACHUTE WOULD BE...

...USELESS IF THERE WERE A FOLLOWING WIND.

AND A PAIR OF IMMOBILISING AND STABILISING...

...ANCHORS ARE NOT THE WAY.

IF ONLY I COULD CUT SOME CORNERS WITH MY RESEARCH...

CUT SOME CORNERS!! EUREKA!!

I'LL REINVENT THE WHEEL -- AND MAKE IT AN OCTO-, HEDRA-, POLYUNSATURATED-, ER, NOT-QUITE-ROUND-ONE.

IF THAT DOESN'T SLOW 'EM DOWN FOR A MILLENNIUM, NOTHING WILL.

MAKE UP A SET OF THESE, CHUCK, AND HIGH-SPEED ROLLERBLADE CRASHES WILL BE A THING OF THE FUTURE...

UG?

...ASK YER CHUM TO EXPLAIN. HE LOOKS THE INTELLECTUAL TYPE...

...MIND YOU, HE APPEARS TO BE BARKING UP THE WRONG TREE...

...CRACKPOT CANINES! NOW HE'S MISSING THE POINT COMPLETELY...

...HE'S NOT MAKING MY REVOLUTIONARY NO-REVOLUTIONS PER SECOND, GO-SLOWER ROLLERBLADE WHEEL...

...HE'S JUST A DOG WHO'S GOT THE WRONG END OF THE STICK. BARK SOME SENSE INTO HIM, GROMIT. GO ON, LAD!

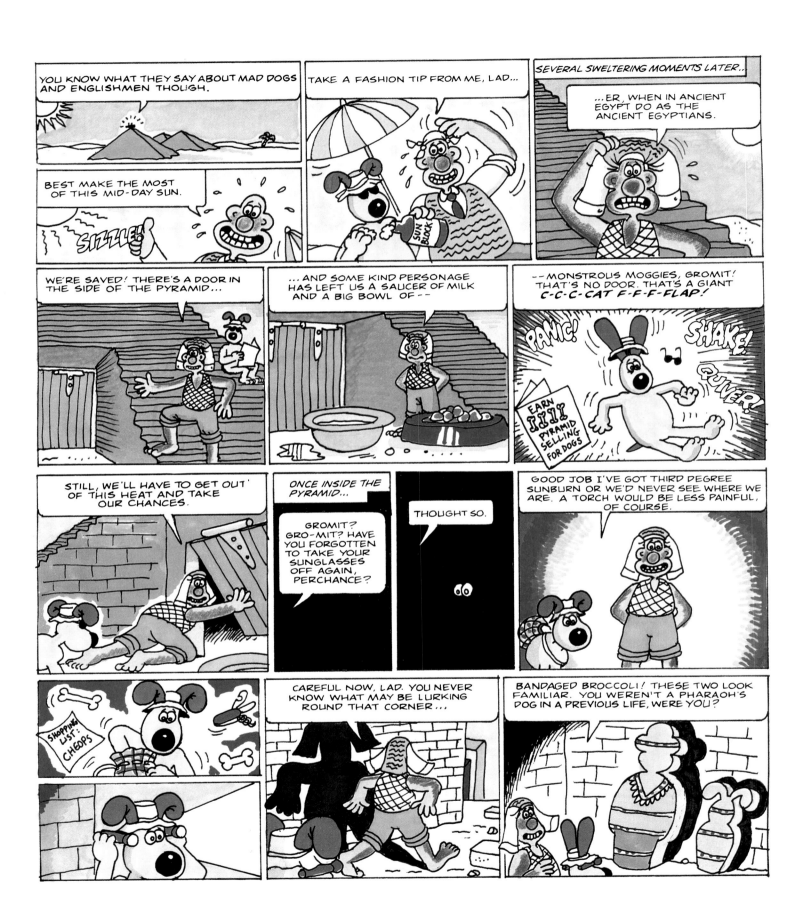

NO TIME FOR SNIFFING OTHER DOGS NOW, GROMIT. WE'VE GOT TO FIND MY SLIPPER.

SNIFF! TWITCH!

FOLLOW ME. WE MAY STUMBLE OVER ANOTHER...

CLUE!

AS I THOUGHT. THESE PYRAMIDS ARE FULL OF SECRET CHAMBERS WHERE A SHOE THIEF MIGHT BURY HIS TREASURES.

DON'T MIND THESE CHUMPS. THEY'RE ONLY STATUES TO SCARE OFF THE GULLIBLE.

BLINK!

SHIFTY STARE!

'COURSE IF THEY *WERE* REAL THEY COULD PROBABLY GIVE YOU A VERY NASTY NIP...

MY, WHAT HEAVY PAWS YOU HAVE ALL OF A SUDDEN, GROMIT.

TAP! TAP!

AND IF YOU DON'T MIND MY SAYING SO, IT'S TIME YOU CUT YOUR FINGERNAILS.

VERTIGINOUS VET'S BILLS!!! A M-M-MYTHOLOGICAL, EGYPTOLOGICAL...

... ORNITHOLOGICAL THINGUMMY. WITH LEGS. AND HE'S NOT ON A LEAD!!!

GRRRR

HE SEEMS TO BE TAKING US SOMEWHERE, GROMIT.

PERHAPS IT'S TO SEE HIS PHARAOH...

...AND IF WE DO MEET ROYALTY, WHATEVER YOU DO, DON'T FORGET TO BOW-WOW.

THE LANDING WAS BUMPY -- BUT AT LEAST WE DIDN'T BECOME THE IN-FLIGHT MEAL.

INSIDE THE PHARAOH'S PALACE...

THAT'S NEFER-TI-TI-TEA-FOR-TWO-TU-TANKHA -- THAT'S THE PHARAOH AND HIS MISSUS, THAT IS.

SORRY, LAD. THE ANCIENT EGYPTIANS WERE INCORRIGIBLE CAT FANCIERS, I'M AFRAID.

WE'D BETTER EXPLAIN WE WEREN'T ROBBING THE PYRAMID. I'LL DO A DRAWING. IT'S THE ONLY LANGUAGE THESE PEOPLE UNDERSTAND.

PARLEZ-VOUS HIEROGLYPHICS, ANY-ONE? WE'RE SLIPPER-HUNTERS FROM THE FUTURE!

I THINK PHARAOH'S GOT THE MESSAGE. AND NOW HE'S TELLING US ABOUT HIS FAMOUS PRISONS...

... AND, ER, HOW HE'S GOING TO LOCK US UP AND THROW AWAY THE KEY -- *HELP!!!*

CHIN UP, CHUCK. COULD BE WORSE. THEY MIGHT HAVE MADE US SLAVES AND HAD US WORKING LIKE, WELL, LIKE DOGS.

MOMENTS LATER...

EH, UP. SOMEONE'S COME TO TAKE YOU WALKIES.

ER, GROMIT WON'T BE NEEDING *TWO* COLLARS. HE'S GOT AN 'O' LEVEL IN OBEDIENCE.

JUST A MINUTE! THIS IS AGAINST THE GENEVA CONVENTION, THIS IS! YOU'LL BE HEARING FROM MY SOLICITOR!

ALL SMELLS VERY FISHY TO ME, LAD.

A TIN OPENER? WHERE ARE WE GOING WITH THAT?

NOUVELLE CUISINE! THEY'VE GOT US FEEDING THE PHARAOH'S CATS. THAT'S A DOG'S LIFE, THAT IS.

18

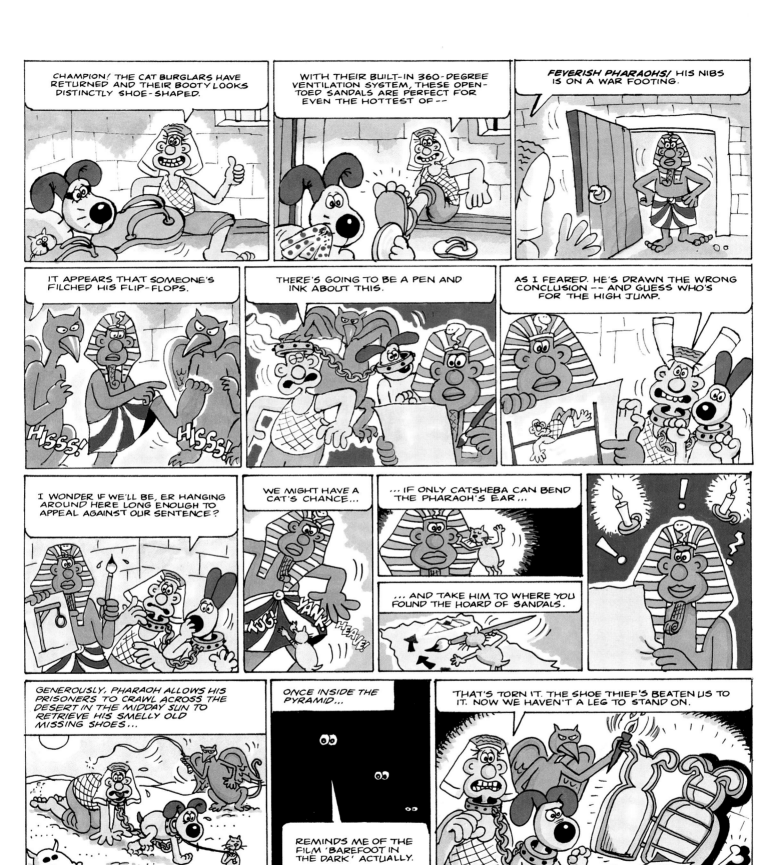

19

MAKE THAT: PREPARE TO CRASH LAND!

A TRIFLE PAINFUL ON RE-ENTRY, AS THEY SAY.

KER-PLONK! THUD! OUCH! SQUISH!

YOU'D BETTER TAKE MY LONGLIFE CARPET CLOGS UNTIL WE GET YOUR SANDALS BACK. OH, AND ANOTHER THING, YOUR PHARAOH-NESS...

...WE'LL NEED A RIGHT ROYAL BUMP-START!

CHOCKS AWA-A-A-A-Y, CHUCK!

CRUMBLE! SPARK! RATTLE! BUMP! BOUNCE!

GOOD JOB THE SHOE THIEF IS CRACKERS ABOUT WENSLEYDALE -- HIS CHEESE WRAPPERS WILL LEAD US STRAIGHT TO MY SLIPPER!

BETTER GIVE IT SOME EXTRA WELLY, GROMIT.

SLOW DOWN, LAD! I'M AGEING DISGRACEFULLY.

SPEED UP AGAIN! I'VE COME OVER ALL IMMATURE.

I'LL TAKE THE CONTROLS NOW, THANK YOU! THEN AT LEAST WE'LL ENJOY A SMOOTH--

CRASH! BANG! WALLOP!

DANGEROUS DÉJÀ-VUS! THIS LOOKS STRANGELY FAMILIAR. I WONDER WHY THE SHOE THIEF BROUGHT US HERE?

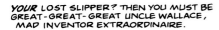

YOUR LOST SLIPPER? THEN YOU MUST BE GREAT-GREAT-GREAT UNCLE WALLACE, MAD INVENTOR EXTRAORDINAIRE.

A BIT LESS OF THE 'EXTRA-ORDINAIRE', IF YOU PLEASE. WHERE DID YOU FIND THESE SLIPPERY REMAINS?

SAME PLACE I FOUND THE DUSTY PLANS FOR YOUR GRANDFATHER CLOCK TIME MACHINE: STUFFED BEHIND THE RADIATOR WITH AN OLD BONE.

VIRTUAL CHESS

STUFFED BEHIND THE RADIATOR!!?? GROMIT!!! YOU'RE IN THE DOGHOUSE 'TIL WE SAVE CIVILIZATION FROM THIS HOPPING MAD SHOE SHORTAGE MULARKEY WE'VE CREATED.

FIRST THING IS TO RECREATE THE ORIGINAL COMFY CARPET SLIPPER. HOW'S THE PROTOTYPE?

CUSHIONED ARCH 'N' ANKLE SUPPORT, CHECK. TOE GRIP 'N' HEEL SWIVEL, CHECK. SOLE SLIDE 'N' BALL BOUNCE, CHECK. BUT IT'S STILL NOT COMFY.

DANGER! SLIPPER-TESTING IN PROGRESS

I'LL TELL YOU WHY NOT. IT'S THE WRONG COLOUR! GOT A POT OF RED, GREEN AND YELLOW PAINT, PERCHANCE?

AS EARTH CRACKS UNDER AEONS OF CLOG TRAFFIC...

THE MET OFFICE ISSUED THE FOLLOWING WARNING...

... PEDESTRIANS ARE ADVISED NOT TO APPROACH NORFOLK...

WHICH IS NOW COMPLETELY WORN OUT AND POTENTIALLY DANGEROUS...

TARTAN

CRIKEY! MUST GET THESE SLIPPERS FINISHED...

... RECALL ALL OUR KILLER CARPET CLOGS AND REPLACE THE FOOT-WEAR YOU 'BORROWED' FROM THE TIME-SPACE CONTINUUM.

WONDER HOW THE TIME MACHINE REPAIRS ARE GOING?

BANG!
BANG
BANG!
KEEP OUT DOGS AT WORK

FAN-SLIPPER-TASTIC, LADS! AND AN ONBOARD DIGITAL DISPLAY GIZMO TO BOOT!

2096
WG 1

THE FUTURE IS ALL BEHIND US NOW AND THE PAST AHEAD -- LET OPERATION CLOG DAMAGE LIMITATION BEGIN!

2096
WG 1

WE'LL BE AT THE BATTLE OF HASTINGS ANY YEAR NOW—HOPEFULLY IN TIME TO STOP KING HAROLD PUTTING HIS FOOT IN IT.

OI! HAROLD, CHUCK. THOSE CLOGS WE LENT YOU ARE LIFE-THREATENING! WATCH OUT!

TRY THESE FOR SIZE AND PASS 'EM ROUND.

AAAAGGHHH!

HOT FOOTING IT BACK TO THE ICE AGE...

THESE COMFY SLIPPERS SHOULD GET MAN'S FUTURE TRANSPORTATION NEEDS OFF ON THE RIGHT FOOT...

...AND FAST FORWARDING TO ANCIENT EGYPT.

AND HERE'S A PAIR I MADE LATER FOR YOU AND QUEEN NEFER-TI-TEA-FOR-TWO-TU-TU... FOR YOU AND MRS PHARAOH.

THAT'S CLOG DAMAGE NIPPED IN THE BUD. EVERYTHING'S SLIPPER-SHAPED AND BRISTOL FASHION. HOME, GROMIT—AND DON'T SPARE THE HORSEPOWER!

WEST WALLABY STREET, THE PRESENT...

AT LAST! AND JUST IN TIME FOR CHEESE!

AND A SAUCER OF MILK...

SEEMS WE'VE AN ANCIENT EGYPTIAN STOWAWAY.

AS I ALWAYS SAY. HAPPINESS IS A WEDGE OF WENSLEYDALE...

...AND A PAIR OF ERGONOMICALLY DESIGNED COMFY CARPET SLIPPERS. IN TARTAN, OF COURSE.

SUFFERING SAVELOYS! I CAN FEEL A DISTINCT DRAUGHT IN THE ANKLE DEPARTMENT.

YOU HAVEN'T SEEN MY OTHER SOCK, PERCHANCE?

THE CURSE OF THE RAMSBOTTOMS

NIL DESPERANDUM, CHUCK!
(Which, along with *Per ardua ad Asda*, a traditional greeting at Roman supermarkets, is the only bit of Latin Wallace knows)

WALLACE
Inventor, handyman and gentleman motorcyclist, Wallace nurses a passion for the cheese of the Wensleydale region, and a tendresse for another local delicacy – the pulchritudinous Miss Wendolene Ramsbottom.

GROMIT
Bon viveur, bibliophile and barker, Wallace's constant travelling companion on the motorcycle is currently scripting a remake of Tennessee Williams' classic, *A Sidecar Named Desire*. Gromit's interest in bones remains undimmed, however. He is, after all, still a dog.

MISS WENDOLENE RAMSBOTTOM
Was there ever a maiden so fair as Wendolene, former wool shop proprietor and now the chatelaine of Ramsbottom Hall on 't' Ramsbottom Moor? Quite possibly there was – but not in this story there isn't.

PRESTON
Originally a cyber-dog created by Daddy, Wendolene's late father, Preston is undergoing modification as part of an ongoing series of improvements. Currently a cyber-butler powered by a rechargeable 12-volt car battery, everything is tickety-boo – except, that is, his voice control box which still suff. Ers. Tee. Thing. Probl. Ems. You get the pic. Ture.

RHETT LEICESTER
Charming, suave, debonair and sophisticated are just four of the flattering adjectives no-one in their right mind will ever apply to Rhett Leicester. An international cheese magnate, and Wendolene's lodger, Rhett's hobbies include garden gnomes and, er, garden gnomes.

BILL 'CHEESY' CHEESEMAN
* NOTE FROM THE PUBLISHERS: Due to circumstances beyond our control, no illustration is available of Mr Bill Cheeseman, Wensleydale's master cheesemaker. As you will read on the next page, he is currently missing on Ramsbottom Moor. We sincerely hope he turns up before the end of the story, and apologise for your temporary loss of picture.

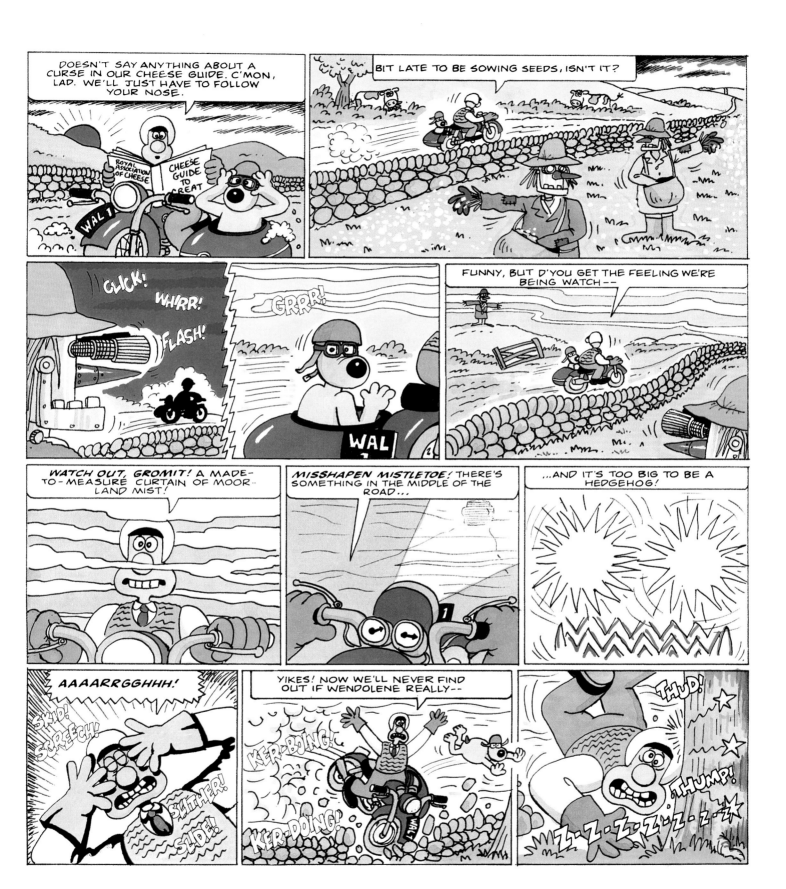

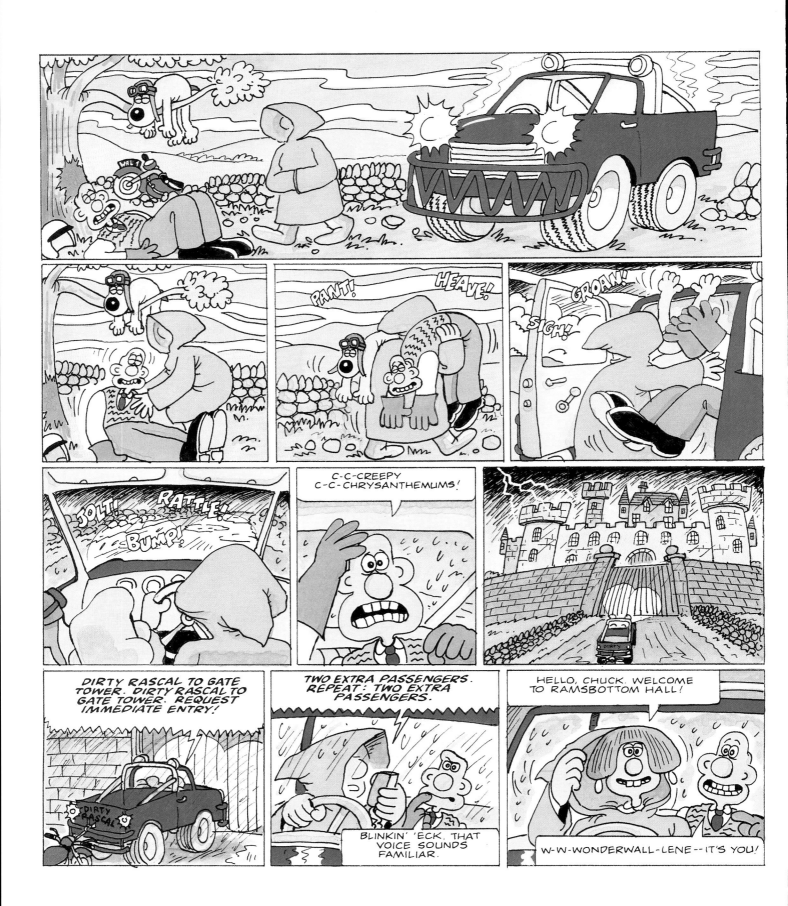

34

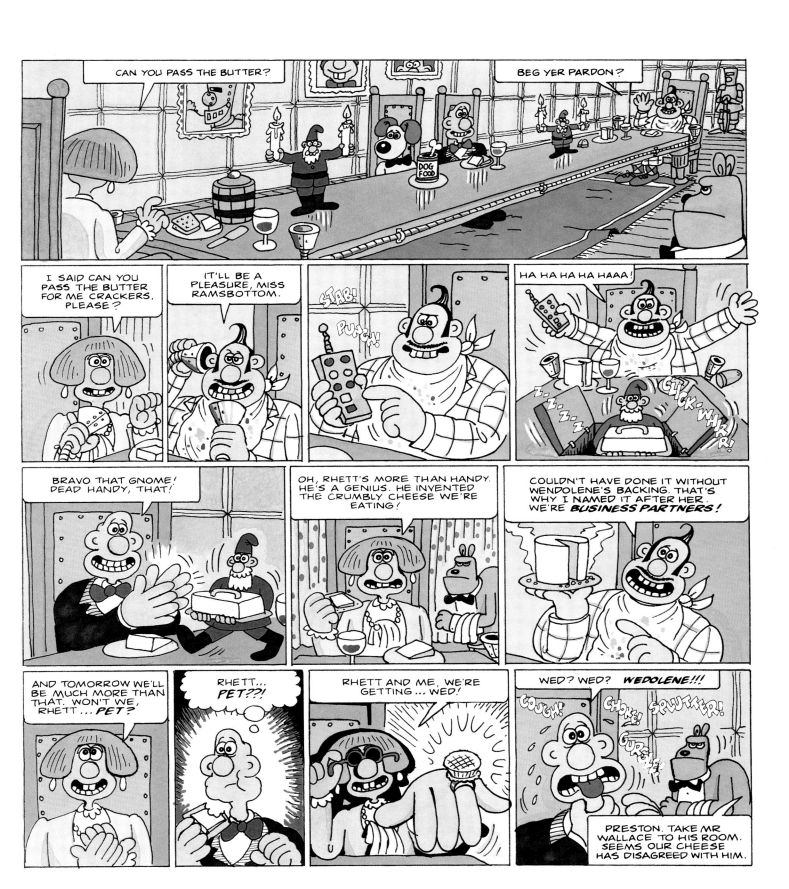

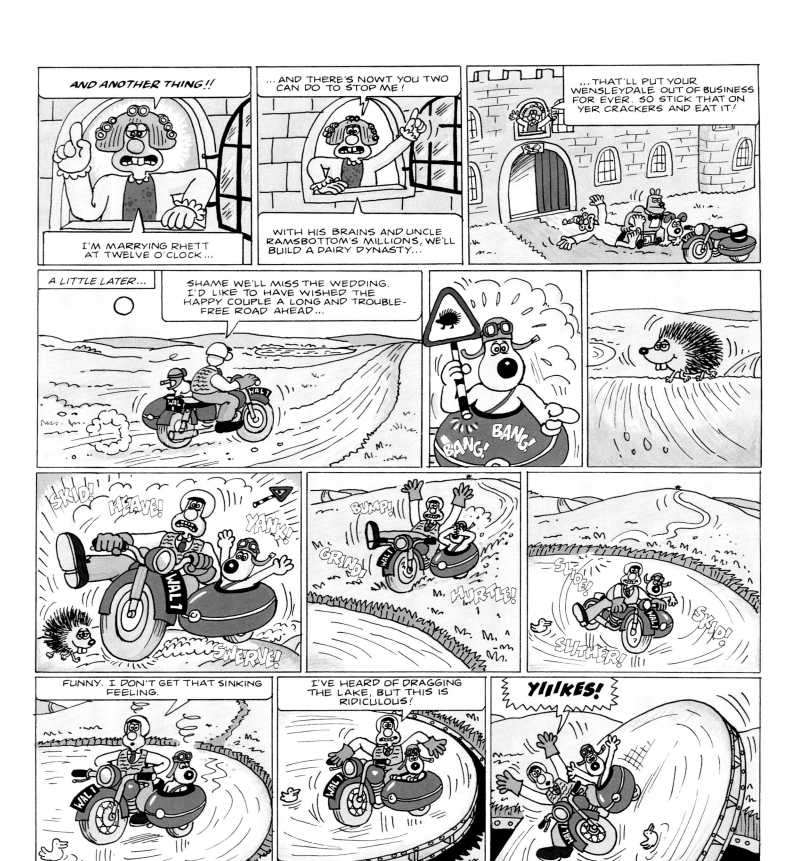

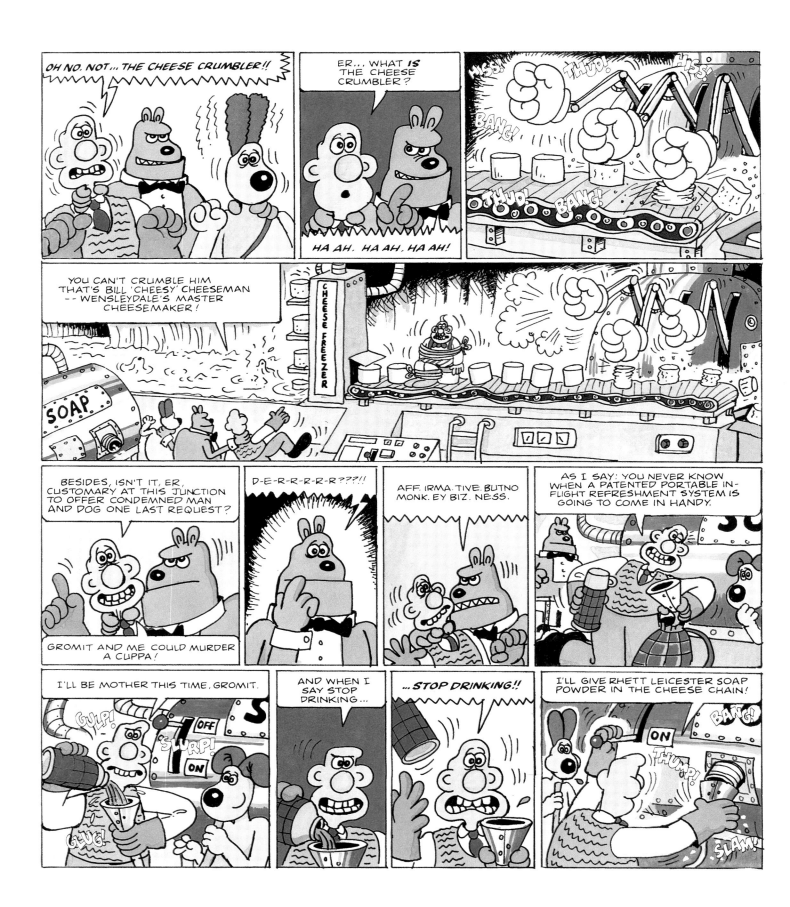

40

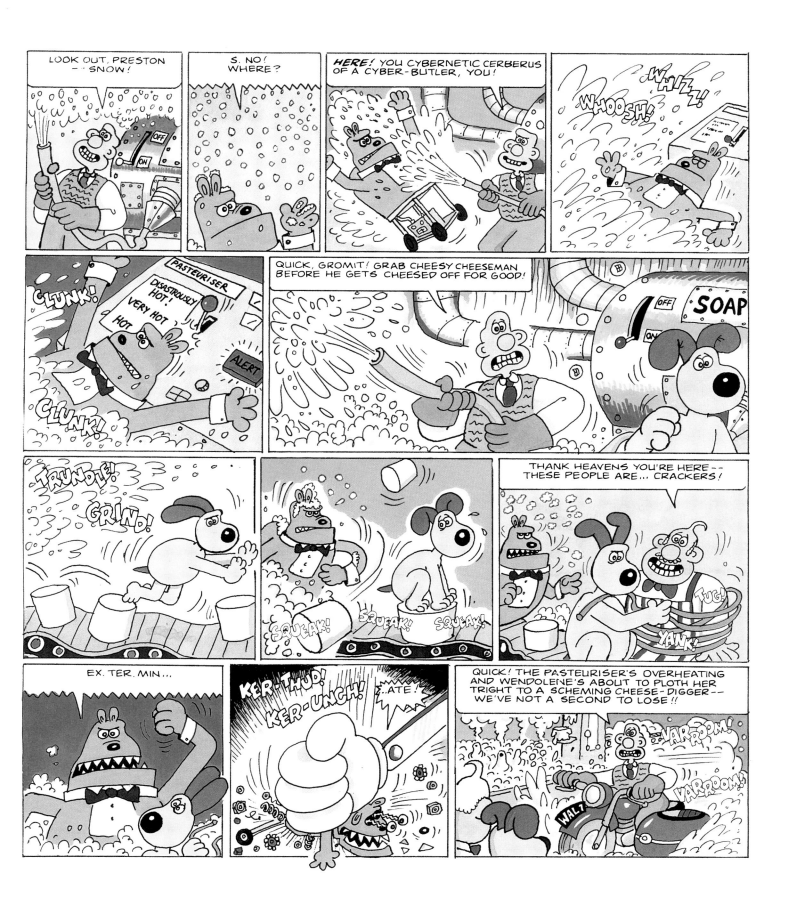

41

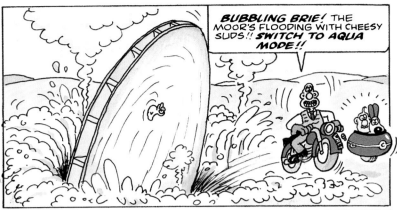

43